Ye New Spell Book

Brian Moses lives in Sussex with his wife and two daughters. He travels the country presenting his poems in schools and libraries. He also wishes it to be known that neither he, nor his editor, will accept responsibility for anything made to disappear, or for any nasty objects or creatures that are conjured up, through meddling with the spells in this book. Heed this warning and take care when reading aloud.

Alan Rowe has been working as an illustrator for the last sixteen years, having taken a degree in drawing silly pictures at Kingston University. He lives in Sutton, Surrey with a partner who also draws silly pictures, three children, two cats, two goldfish and a room full of robots.

D0994990

Ye New Spell Book

Magical Poems
Chosen by Brian Moses

Illustrated by Alan Rowe

MACMILLAN CHILDREN'S BOOKS

First published 2002
by Macmillan Children's Books
a division of Macmillan Publishers Limited
20 New Wharf Road, London N1 9RR
Basingstoke and Oxford
www.panmacmillan.com

Associated companies throughout the world

ISBN 0 330 39708 7

5 7 9 8 6

A CIP catalogue record for this book is available from the British Library.

Printed by Mackays of Chatham plc, Chatham, Kent.

'A Charm for Sweet Dreams' by Wes Magee first published in *The Phantom's
Fant-Tastic Show*, OUP, 2000.

'Spell for the End of Term' by Matt Simpson first published in *The Pigs'
Thermal Underwear*, Headland, 1994.

'Spell of the Bridge' by Helen Lamb first published in *Going up Ben Nevis
in a Bubble Car*, ASLS, 2000.

Contents

On Reflection

Don't practise strange spells in front of the mirror,

don't point at yourself, with a wand;

don't practise strange spells in front of the mirror,

I did – now I live in this pond.

Mike Johnson

For My Father

Oh,
But if there was a spell
To bring my father back
I would gather its components at once.
His watch, still ticking,
His old, grey, baggy jumper
A photograph of his smile
A compass and a candle.

I would whisper the spell late into the night
I would say it loud, shout it, sing it
The whole world and his neighbour
Would hear me singing

Ah,
But there is no spell
To bring him back
Only the sun rising in the East
And a prayer
For a new beginning.

Roger Stevens

The Goalie's Curse on the Other Team's Striker

May your shorts lose their elastic,
May your trainers lose a lace,
May you slip and slide and slither,
Falling flat upon your face.

May your legs turn into porridge,
May your feet turn into lead.
May a million mosquitoes
Take a tea break on your head.

May a dragon singe your socks,
May you be swallowed by a whale.
May a squad car full of coppers
Come and drag you off to jail.
May you fall into a pit
Dug by a massive, mutant mole.
And may all those curses strike you NOW!
Before you reach my goal!

Paul Bright

The Dragon's Curse

Enter darkness. Leave the light.
Here be nightmare. Here be fright.
Here be dragon, flame and flight.
Here be spit-fire. Here be grief.
So curse the bones of unbelief.
Curse the creeping treasure-thief.
Curse much worse the dragon-slayer.
Curse his purse and curse his payer.
Curse these words. Preserve their sayer.
Earth and water, fire and air.
Prepare to meet a creature rare.
Enter, now, if you dare.
Enter, now . . . the dragon's lair!

Nick Toczek

How to Turn a Class Hamster into a Dinosaur

First, prepare your hamster
for life as a ferocious, school-eating dinosaur.
Show it pictures of what life was like
when dinosaurs roamed the earth.
(Ask a teacher.)
Next, motivate it.
Give it lessons on how to scare teachers.
(Diagrams may help.)
Get some prehistoric gooey stuff,
from places unexplored in millions of years . . .
(if your brother has his own room,
it is always a good idea to start looking there.)
Smear this gunk on the walls
of the school you want chomped
whilst chanting:
Teachers run and scream and stumble
make a tasty red brick crumble!
Make a giant dino gangsta!
Megasaurus Biggus Hampsta!

Repeat until satisfied.
You now have your very own
Turbosaurus Hamster-beast.

Feed carefully.

Matt Lees

Spell to Banish a Pimple

Get back, pimple
get back to where you belong

Get back to never-never land
and I hope you stay there long

Get back, pimple
get back to where you belong

How dare you take up residence
in the middle of my face

I never offered you a place
beside my dimple

Get back, pimple
get back to where you belong

Get packing, pimple
I banish you to outer space

If only life was that simple

John Agard

Instant Room Tidy Spell

Say:
'Make my mother's eyes go misty
when she walks into my room.'
Say:
'Fill the atmosphere with fog
so it's hard to see in the gloom.'
Say:
'Fix it for everything to return
at once to its rightful place.'
Say:
'Lift the gloom.'

Now see a smile
spread over your mother's face.

Brian Moses

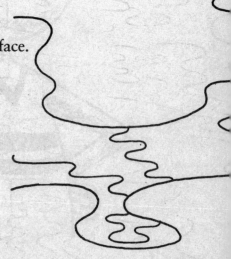

Three Love Charms

Regular
Strength

You're knock-out pretty,
You're smart and witty
And though I'm zitty
Will you go out with me?

Extra
Strength

You may ride my bike,
If that's what you'd like,
While beside I hike –
Will you go out with me?

Super-
charged

I will give you gold,
Give you cash to fold,
Give you wealth untold –
Will you go out with me?

If the love charms are to be intoned to a boy change the
Regular Strength to:

You are drop-dead cute,
You're a handsome brute,
And though I'm no beaut –
Will you go out with me?

Philip Waddell

A Guaranteed
Cure for All Curses

Anybody knows
that the way to cure a curse,
any curse at all,
is to whistle it away.

It doesn't matter what sort:
loud and bossy
hip-hoppy
chirpy-cheerful
under-the-breath
couldn't-care-less
Any sort of whistle will do.

It doesn't matter where:
creepy underpasses
windy hilltops
gloomy alleyways
gingham precincts
golden beaches
Any place is OK.

It doesn't matter when:
wakey-wakey-time
take-a-break-time
all-alone-time
pals-together-time
the midnight witching hour
Any time is fine.

So that's it, dead simple.
It works every time.
Of course –
      first you've got to know
        how to whistle.

Patricia Leighton

How to Make the World a Better Place

Firstly, take a large amount of *love*
(the larger the amount the better)
and a generous portion of *sympathy*.
Blend together.

Next add lashings of *patience*
and heaps of *consideration*.
Stir, then set aside.

Now take *understanding*
and peel away any *prejudice*
(this latter should be thrown away).
Finely chop into small pieces.

Squeeze the juice of *loyalty*
and grate the rind of *honesty*,
then add both these and *understanding*
to the mixture.

Season with *hope*.

Heat gently, stirring well.
Do not allow to boil.

Once mixture has warmed right through
remove from heat
and drain away any remaining *hatred*
and *cruelty*.

Finally, sprinkle with *smiles*
and garnish with *laughter*.

Makes enough for everyone.

Gillian Floyd

Spell to Help Turn You into the Teacher's Pet

Take 100 grams of very expensive presents
bought specially for your teacher on the most
   unexpected occasions.
Add a sprinkle of neat notes spread with hearts and
   hard sums
to be slipped on to your teacher's desk at lunchtimes.
Pop in several trophies with inscriptions that say:
"You're the best teacher in the whole wide world and
   beyond."

Stir in a pinch of extra homework that isn't set yet
along with 20 grams of gossipy girly laughter
reserved only for your teacher's jokes.
Slowly slip in a hundred hints about being top in class
and about having extra peeps at SATS papers before
    the big day.
Add 80 grams of extra comments in class discussions,
and to round it off nicely, a shower of tears when you
    move up a class.

Karen and Brian Moses

Growing Spell

Take a handful of dust from a skyscraper's roof
A teaspoon of clippings from a giraffe's left hoof
And a packet of sunflower seed
That's all you need.
Take them all
Swallow
Grow tall

John Coldwell

Spells

I crackle and spit. I lick and leap higher.
This is the spell of the raging fire.

I clasp and grasp. I grip in a vice.
This is the spell of torturing ice.

I claw and scratch. I screech and I wail.
This is the spell of the howling gale.

I clash and I crash. I rip asunder.
This is the spell of booming thunder.

I whisper. I stroke. I tickle the trees.
This is the spell of the evening breeze.

I slither. I slide. I drift and I dream.
This is the spell of the murmuring stream.

John Foster

Spell to Bring a Smile

Come down, Rainbow
Rainbow, come down

I have a space for you
in my small face

If my face is too small for you
take a space in my chest

If my chest is too small for you
take a space in my belly

If my belly is too small for you
then take every part of me

Come down, Rainbow
Rainbow, come down

You can eat me from head to toe

John Agard

A Spell to Cure Sorrow and Create Joy

Take the whisper of the river,
The thunder of the sea,
The echo of the songbird,
The rustle of the tree,
The howling of the blizzard,
The purring of the cat,
The shudder of the earthquake,
The whistle of the gnat,
The rumble of the storm cloud,
The singing of the sun,
The music of the moonrise,
And mix them, one by one,
Till all the notes are silver
And all the chords are gold,

Then give your gift of laughter
To the sick, the sad, the old.

Clare Bevan

Curse All Bullies

For bullies who hurt
with words that sting,
make them afraid
of harmless things.

May slugs keep them from their sleep,
May flies make their flesh creep;
May shadows give them a fearful shock,
May nits make their knees knock;
May starlings stand their hair on end,
May dragonflies drive them round the bend . . .

May butterflies betray them,
May damselflies dismay them.

May Sunday make them sad,
May Monday drive them mad;
May Tuesday give them a terrible time,
May Wednesday make them whine;
May Thursday give them tears,
May Friday give them fears;
May Saturday cause them pain,
Looking forward to Sunday again.

May frogs give them a fright,
May toads turn their hair white;
May chickens give them a chill,
May warts destroy their will;
May scabs make them scared,
May ducks make them despair;
May worms make them worry,
May hamsters make them hurry.

May snails subdue them,
May bugs bugaboo them.

For bullies who hurt
with words that sting,
make them all afraid
of harmless things.

Mike Jubb

The Wizard Said:

"You find a sheltered spot that faces south . . ."
"And then?"
"You sniff and put two fingers in your mouth . . ."
"And then?"
"You close your eyes and roll your eyeballs round . . ."
"And then?"
"You lift your left foot slowly off the ground . . ."
"And then?"
"You make your palm into a kind of cup . . ."
"And then?"
"You very *quickly* raise your right foot up . . ."
"And then?"
"You fall over."

Richard Edwards

How to Get Rid of a Wart

Grindle a sprig of wallaby-weed.
Squake it into flintersticks.
Flib a grib of grubbery seed
Craddled over crindlerix.
Pragg a skib of twenty choggs.
Splinchify for chortlequart
Glamped inside the brindlebogs.
Now, without a second thought,
Rub it on to clear the wart.

Celia Warren

Spell for Sleeping Soundly

Do a good deed by daylight
Expecting no reward
Give to a charity
One penny more than you can afford
Forgive from the heart
And put right a wrong that you have done
Then you will sleep soundly
From the setting until the rising of the sun

Roger Stevens

A Quick Chant for Keeping You Safe at Halloween

Hobgoblins and spellbinders,
Angels in rags,
Liar or truthteller,
Lacewitch or hag,
Over the gristle bones,
Warlocks fight,
Earwigs are flying with
Elfin and sprite.
Now keep me safe this Halloween night!

Mary Green

Spell to Silence a Sister

Cachala chachala
Flix-flax-flox
Titter-tatter flitter-flatter
Chitter-chatterbox!

Cachala chachala
Flix-flax-flop
Titter-tatter all day long
Chitter-chatter STOP!

Judith Nicholls

Note: Chachalacha in Mexican Spanish is a grouse or any bird that cries continually as it flies; colloquially, a chatterbox!

Recipe for a Dragon

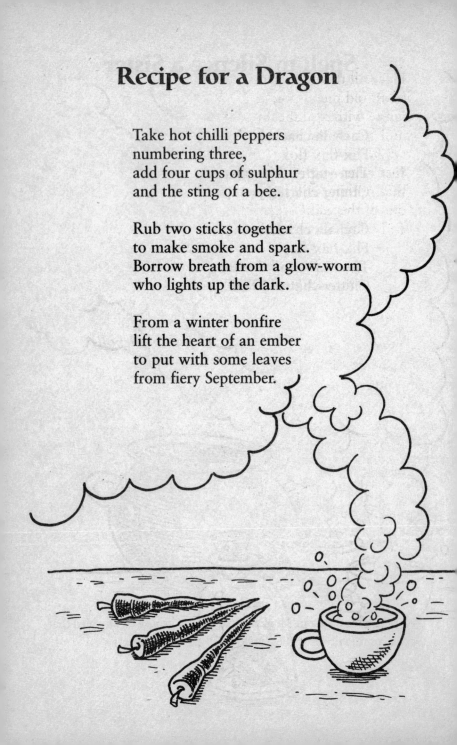

Take hot chilli peppers
numbering three,
add four cups of sulphur
and the sting of a bee.

Rub two sticks together
to make smoke and spark.
Borrow breath from a glow-worm
who lights up the dark.

From a winter bonfire
lift the heart of an ember
to put with some leaves
from fiery September.

Place all the ingredients
in an old metal pot,
ignite with a sunbeam
and stir up the lot.

Just when you're thinking
that nothing will happen,
out of the white steam
will come a small dragon.

Robin Mellor

Spell for the End of Term

Who is it says that spells don't work?
Whoever it is Look Out!
I made one up last Saturday
That should leave you in no doubt.

I said the alphabet backwards,
Boiled up a magic brew
Of things you dare not mention.
Bet you wished you knew!

Well, sort of things like bat-spit,
And hairs from a pharaoh's chin,
Some bits of twine, some old red wine,
And one white shark's black fin!

When Mum and Dad went to Sainsbury's
To get the shopping done,
I climbed into our attic
To have a bit of fun.

So look out, Mrs Faraday,
Who shouts at us in class:
At ten past two next Friday
be turned into an ass!

With long grey ears all hairy
And a screechy loud hee-haw.
It's – before we go on holiday –
My present to Class Four!

Matt Simpson

Invocation to Be Used When Thinking up Excuses

May my tongue be golden as the sun
And words flow from my mouth
In streams of silver charms.

May my thoughts be quick as a cheetah
Sharp as a fox.
May they twist and turn
Sinuous and smooth as a snake.

May my face shine with innocence
My wide eyes tell sweet lies.

From top to toe may I glow
Yellow as butter
That will never melt.

Patricia Leighton

Spell for a Sneak

May icicles stick in your throat
And all your eyelashes fall out
Your favourite foods taste like sand
Hideous boils despoil each hand
And friends forsake you one by one
If you should tell what I have done

Peggy Poole

Spell to Make Your Teacher Disappear

From the blackboard gather chalk-dust,
Mix it with a drop of ink,
Put it in an empty paint-pot
Rinsed out at the staff-room sink.

Stir it gently with a ruler,
Let it bubble till it's thick.
Make a pair of magic passes
O'er it with a metre stick.

Gently chant the eight times table
Backwards down to eight times one;
Leave it now to gather power –
Soon the magic will be done.

As the hometime bell is ringing
Cringe and wait in fright and fear:
Watch your teacher put her coat on . . .
Watch! – and soon she'll disappear!

S. J. Saunders

Granny's Old Wives' Cures
for the Cold

Place old sweaty socks on a radiator,
turn up the heat, position nose next to it
and smell for two hours.

Soak snail shells and coils of earthworm
for two days in lemon juice and boiled water
then swallow in one go.

Lie in a bath full of freezing cold sea water,
blackberry juice and crushed egg shells,
wearing only a swimming costume and suitable goggles.

Take shavings of a moustache, toe nail clippings,
pencil sharpenings, an egg cup of morning dew
and a dash of vinegar, then pour over your head.

Grill four mushrooms and two garden slugs
on a bed of fresh grass and flower oil.
Best to sprinkle with chewed dandelions.

Add the sweat of a sheep's brow, two raw eggs
and three spots of a black ladybird
then rub into your hair and leave overnight.

Ian Souter

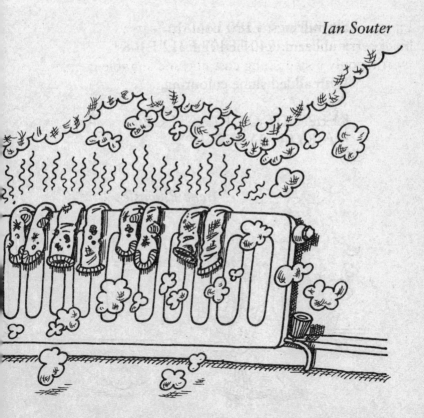

The Witch's Bad Luck Brew

Ingredients:
Dried toads' eggs 50.0mg
Ground wings of bats 30.0mg
Extract of adders' tongues 10.0mg
Modified beetle juice 5.0mg
Wasp stings (emulsified) 00.5mg

Iron supplement:
contains hydrogenated wireworms.

Flavourings: E100 E160(b)
Stablizers: E401 E407 E412 E466

With added slime colouring.

KEEP OUT OF REACH OF
EVERYBODY EXCEPT . . .

Irene Rawnsley

Spelling Test

A spell to turn someone into a striped horse-like creature . . . **Zebracadabra**

Spell to change someone into a clawed, sideways walking crustacean . . . **Crabracadabra**

Spell to do your shopping for you . . . **Asda**cadabra

Spell that takes pictures . . . Abrada**camera**

Spell that makes you hiss and writhe on your belly . . .
Abrada**cobra**

Spell that lights up a very old-fashioned and well-to-do ballroom . . . Abra**candelabra**

Spell that bashes your sister . . . Abrada**clobberer**

Spell that bashes your brother . . . Abrada**clobberim**

Spell that makes your teacher cross . . . Abra**mad**abra

Spell to make you cheerful . . . Abra**glad**abra

Really rude underwear spell . . . **Abracadabra**

Spell to make you fall over . . . *Izzy whizzy let's get dizzy*

Bubbling frothing spell . . . *Izzy whizzy let's get fizzy*

Spell that interrupts the poet halfway through a wo**SHAZAM**rd.

Paul Cookson

Spell of the Bridge

Hold the wish on your tongue
As you cross
What the bridge cannot hear
Cannot fall

For the river would carry
Your hopes to the sea
To the net of a stranger
To the silt bed of dreams

Hold the wish on your tongue
As you cross

And on the far side
Let the wish go first.

Helen Lamb

Teenage Sisters

'Sugar and spice
and all things nice'
may be what *little* girls
are made of,
    but
teenage sisters are made of
    ACID!

Would an Everest of sugar
sweeten an adolescent?
Would all the spice in India
make my sister pleasant?
With a waterfall of syrup
and the whole of Asia's spice,
I doubt if even all of that
would make *my* sister nice.

So give me the sweetness of angels,
and the spice of Shangri-la;
add the smiles of a billion babies,
and the light of a billion stars;
give me the fun of a puppy at play
and stir with a hurricane,
then soak my sister in Love and Peace,
and make her human again.

Mike Jubb

A Recycled Recipe for Turning Your Enemy into a Beetle

(the original recipe dates right back to Shakespeare's day)

Unfortunately, the traditional ingredients
are now politically incorrect
so, for eye of newt, substitute eye of prawn
and for toe of frog, a pig's trotter will have to do.
As for fillet of a fenny snake,
try a nice fillet of haddock instead.
It's no use looking for wool of bat.
The little wretches are a protected species these days.
Wool of hamster will suffice.
Just snip some off with your mother's nail scissors.
Tongue of dog is another valuable ingredient
now frowned upon.

Use a piece of spam, a poor substitute
but better than nothing.
Now, for lizard's leg
use the legs of about twenty daddy long legs.
They are always dropping off
so can be used without offending anybody.
Don't use howlet's wing
or you will be arrested.
It makes me long for the good old days
when howlets' wings
could be had by the cartload.
Go to the freezer and remove
a dozen chicken wings.
An essential ingredient
used to be tiger entrails
but as the tiger is even more
endangered than the bat,
we must improvise.

Once more, the humble chicken
comes to our rescue.
Six sets of giblets
will serve your purpose.
We would like to have used
root of hemlock and of mandrake
but you aren't allowed to dig up wild plants
in these miserable modern times,
so go to Grandad's allotment
and dig up some parsnips and radishes.
Then purchase five litres of unicorn's milk
(available at most supermarkets).
Then, standing on a wild and lonely heath
with thunder rumbling and lightning flashing,
light your fire and drop your ingredients
into a briskly bubbling cauldron.
Stir constantly, all the while

pacing round, widdershins,
and chanting the standard spells.
When the mixture has reduced to a thick, grey glue,
extinguish the fire carefully.
(We can't have the blasted heath
catching fire, can we?)
A dab of the mixture on your victim's chair should do
    the trick.
And remember, do not step on the beetle.
Such practices have been forbidden by the European
    Human Rights Act.

Note
Whatever you do, do not substitute cows' milk
for that of the unicorn even though it is cheaper.
The mammoth that miserly Mother Mumble
created carried her off never to be seen again.
(Miserly Mother Mumble, not the mammoth.
The mammoth is still terrorizing Chipping Ongar.)

Marian Swinger

Casting a Spell on
Old Charlie Bell

Now I'll cast many a spell on old Charlie Bell
  'cos he didn't play fair and he cheated.
And although I'm a sport from the King's own court
  these spells will be overheated.

By the hem of his coat may he fall from his boat
  and get eaten by forty fishes.
May he take a new job to make a few bob
and end up washing the dishes.

May he fall downstairs and be eaten by bears
  when he wakes on Friday morning.
Let him slip on an eel, become a crocodile's meal
  without a word of warning.

May his bed become soggy and his carpets all boggy
  when a flood pours over his floor.
May he never be warm and a hurricane storm
  blow a tree right through his door.

By the sole of his shoes may a huge kangaroo
  chase him miles across the outback.
May a bat bite his toes and a rat steal his nose
  and never ever give his snout back.

May every black goblin from here to old Dublin
  plague him in sleep or awake.
May he work in all weathers, be tickled by feathers
  and his eyeballs baked in a cake.

May a ghost from a grave give his head a close shave
    and throw all his hair in the ocean.
And may an old banshee from the town of Dundee
    feed him a poisonous potion.

May a troop of red ants creep into his pants
    and cause him to scream and scratch.
May a firework rocket go off in his pocket
    next time he lights a match.

May he shake and shiver when he falls in the river,
  and let a crab swim into his mouth.
May he plunge in a pool on his way home from school
  and the current carry him south.

John Rice

How to Write a Spell

First you must find a magic place.
A haunted room
At the very top of a crumbling tower
Where ivy leaves tap the windows
And cobwebs cling to the bare stones.
Or a hollow tree
At the very centre of a silent wood
Where even the birds whisper
And insects flicker like tiny jewels.
Or an echoing cave
At the very heart of a misty mountain
Where stalactites hang as sharp as fangs
And the bats flap wings of darkness.

Next you must open your heavy book,
Smooth its creamy pages
And breathe its ancient, mysterious smell.

Now you must capture the words
As they flutter by.
Take a pen as sharp and as swift
As your desire,
Let its plume be plucked from the tail
Of the fiery phoenix,
Let its nib be carved with a blade of blue ice,
Let its ink be mixed from the tears of mermaids
And the blood of a green dragon.

Last, you must write your spell.
Let it soar like the song of a skylark.
Let it repeat and repeat
Like the beat of the rain on shining pebbles.
Let it spin and flow.
When it is finished
You will know.

Then draw a single, intricate line
As a sign to show
The enchantment is set like a trap
To catch your wildest wish.
And if you truly believe,
It shall be so.

Clare Bevan

Spellathon Spell

I'm making a spell to help me learn
a hundred difficult spellings
for the school spellathon.
A spelling spell.
I've torn up a dictionary.
I'm throwing in:
transmogrify and **transmutation**,
transcendency and **transformation**,
vertiginous and **vesicate**,
vicarious and **vanadate** . . .
Special spellings for a spell
to help me spell *exceedingly* well.

Stir and agitate,
liquefy . . .

What the heck –
it's worth a try!

Penny Kent

A Charm Against Witches

Turn your eggshell upside down
Smash it to smithereens.
With a broken boat no witch can bring
Stormy black thoughts to your dreams.

Patricia Leighton

Spell of the Troll

Oh lucky Pot Belly,
Stuffed full of tricks,
On your two stout legs
Stand up for me.

Be my fierce face
When I'm jelly,
Speak up when I'm
Stuck and dumb.

And I will comb
Your dreadful locks
Till they crackle –

Just the way you like.

Helen Lamb

Supermarket Spell

"I'm putting a spell on my mum.
What *I* like
Will go into her trolley.
Straight down past the veg, Mum,
And on to spaghetti and beans . . .
Up the next aisle
To those giant bags
Of Maltesers . . .
Along (No, no eggs)
To the muesli bars . . .
Crisps . . .
Then to lemonade,
Burgers and chips.
Well done, Mum!
Now just head for the checkout –
Blink twice when you've paid.
You will soon feel quite normal!"

Sue Cowling

Four Cures for Doglessness

Turn up TV when the advert with the cute puppy
and the toilet roll comes on.

Leave newspaper articles around saying children
are not getting enough exercise.

Tell next door's cat to deposit headless mice,
voles etc. on the patio.

Invite burglars to visit your street – soon!

Sue Cowling

Teacher, Watch Out!

If I stare at you
You'll develop a twitch

If I ignore you
You'll start to itch

If I look through you
You'll not be heard

If I watch your lips
You'll muddle your words

If I close one eye
You'll feel unsure

If I close two
You'll disappear.

So watch it!

If you set homework
I'll shut my eyes

And you'll be in
For a big surprise

You'll see!

Bernard Young

Mother Merryweather's Love Brew

Take a moonbeam trapped in a crystal jar,
a twinkle snatched from the evening star,
a dewdrop taken from spring's first flower,
and raindrops sneaked from a sudden shower.
Mix the bubbling and sparkling brew.
Who drinks it will be your love most true.

Note
Be sure not a drop is left
to be drunk by a passing ferret.
Mother Pye has been pursued
by a lovesick ferret for three years now
and is suing Mother Merryweather
for all she's got.

Marian Swinger

Spell for a Bigger Moon

(for my daughter who doesn't like the dark)

Because of those things in the night which thump and tap
and tingle your spine with a sudden zap;

because there are vampires and spooks
and evil spells in evil books;

and because I like it in bed but just can't see
what it is that lies beyond the edge of me –

grow, grow dear moon up high,
light, light the owls as they wing through the sky:
banish the raven blackness of night –
be brighter, bolder, bigger and beam silver light!

Tim Pointon

a new shoe spell

higgledy-piggledy
harum-scarum
take my new shoes
then I won't have to wear them

Philip Burton

River Tale

First gather morning rain,
Splash down mountainside,
Tip into rivulets, into tributaries and
Make a river.

Chase downstream fearlessly,
Catch cataracts,
Track eddies, spy leaping fish, then
Subside, yawning.

Now, trail wet toes carelessly,
Take detours,
Flow over flood plain, ripple in the sun,
Linger sleepily

And wait to hear
The lap of water shift across sand,
Crabs scuttle,
The moon spill out of the sea,
Curlews call,
And the river pass from source to estuary.

Mary Green

A Charm for Sweet Dreams

May the Ghost
        lie in its grave.
May the Vampire
        see the light.
May the Witch
        keep to her cave,
and the Spectre
        melt from sight.

May the Wraith
        stay in the wood.
May the Banshee
        give no fright.
May the Ghoul
        begone for good,

and the Zombie
          hasten its flight.
May the Troll
          no more be seen.
May the Werewolf
          lose its bite.
May all Spooks
          and Children Green
fade for ever
          in
                the
                    night . . .

                    Wes Magee

To Make Your Broomstick Fly

Old Mother Pye's Patent Spell

Take feather of owl for silent flight,
feather of wren to make it light,
peregrine's feather to make it swift,
feather of skylark to give it lift
and feather of duck for rainy weather.
Bind with a cobweb all together,
bind into broom head, bind into bristle,
then rub into broomstick dragon's gristle.
Rub well in and say the words,
'Klazzmazazz! Fly like a bird.'

Note
If dragon's gristle can't be found,
a roc's will get you off the ground.
And, to make your Hoover fly,
you'll find this spell will still apply.
Just suck the feathers up instead,
chant the spell and lightly spread
some dodo's grease upon the bag,
to make it fly for witch and hag.

Note
Dodo's grease half-price
only at Mother Pye's Organic Emporium.

Marian Swinger

Spell to Make Mum Smile

Say, Good morning, Mum
You look particularly
Pretty. How about
A nice cup of tea?

Roger Stevens

A Recipe to Make You the Most Successful, Rich, Popular and Good-looking Person in the World

(To be cooked and consumed before noon on the first day of April)

Mix a spoonful of goo
With a gloop of shampoo.
Add six green shoots
Of fresh bamboo.
Mix in toothpaste – just a bit.
Add a scoop of cuckoo spit.
Fry in goose fat. Leave to cool.
Eat it: instant April fool!

Celia Warren

A Wishing Charm

At midnight
take five tiny feathers
from a goldcrest's wing.

At midnight
collect five drops of water
from a bubbling spring.

At midnight
gather starshine
into five green crystal phials.

At midnight
draw the sweetest tones
from five medieval viols.

Bury them all on a mountain high
beneath a rowan tree
and you will be granted your dearest wish
whatever it may be.

Penny Kent

Don't Get Your Knickers in a Twist

Poems chosen by Paul Cookson

Don't Get Your Knickers in a Twist is a riotous collection of poems bursting at the seams with disorderly words, idioms, clichés and wordplay. You'd be daft as a brush to miss this side-splitting verbal jousting. Here's a little something to get the ball rolling . . .

from *Today, I Feel*

Today, I feel as:

> Pleased as PUNCH,
> Fit as a FIDDLE,
> Keen as a KNIFE,
> Hot as a GRIDDLE,
> Bold as BRASS,
> Bouncy as a BALL,
> Keen as MUSTARD,
> High as a WALL,
> Bright as a BUTTON,
> Light as a FEATHER,
> Fresh as a DAISY,
> Fragrant as HEATHER,
> Chirpy as a CRICKET,
> Sound as a BELL,
> Sharp as a NEEDLE . . .

I'M SO HAPPY – I'M JUST LOST FOR WORDS.

Gervase Phinn

A selected list of poetry books available from Macmillan

The prices shown below are correct at the time of going to press. However, Macmillan Publishers reserve the right to show new retail prices on covers which may differ from those previously advertised.

A Nest Full of Stars	0 333 96051 3
Poems by James Berry	£9.99
I Did Not Eat the Goldfish	0 330 39718 4
Poems by Roger Stevens	£3.99
The Fox on the Roundabout	0 330 48468 0
Poems by Gareth Owen	£4.99
The Very Best of Paul Cookson	0 330 48014 6
Poems by Paul Cookson	£3.99
The Very Best of David Harmer	0 330 48190 8
Poems by David Harmer	£3.99
The Very Best of Wes Magee	0 330 48192 4
Poems by Wes Magee	£3.99
Don't Get Your Knickers in a Twist	0 330 39769 9
Poems chosen by Paul Cookson	£3.99

All Macmillan titles can be ordered at your local bookshop
or are available by post from:

**Book Service by Post
PO Box 29, Douglas, Isle of Man IM99 1BQ**

Credit cards accepted. For details:
Telephone: 01624 675137
Fax: 01624 670923

E-mail: bookshop@enterprise.net

Free postage and packing in the UK.
Overseas customers: add £1 per book (paperback)
and £3 per book (hardback)